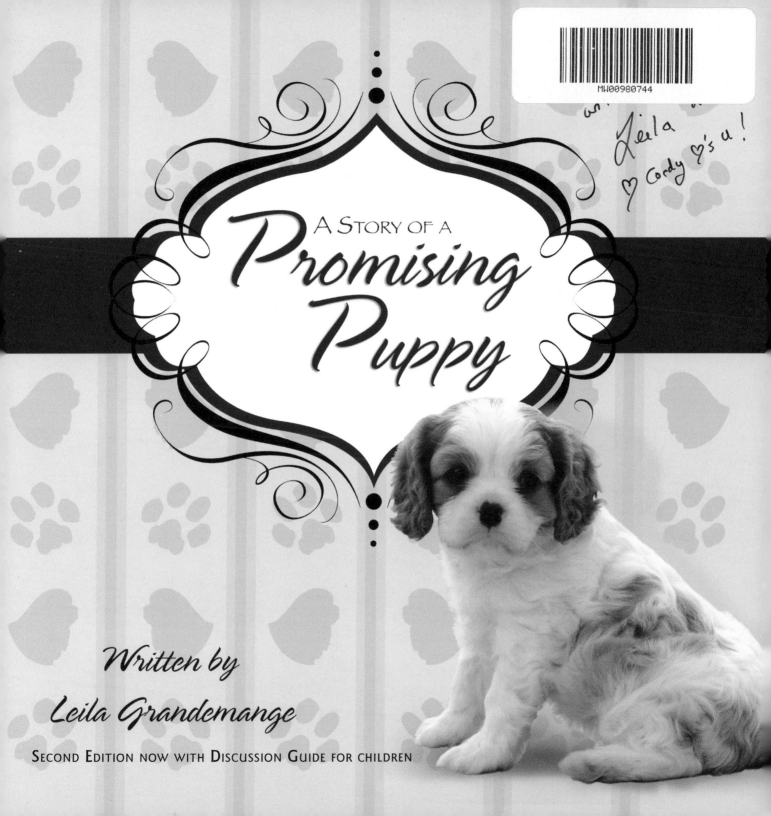

A STORY OF A

Promising
Puppy

Written by

Leila Grandemange

SECOND EDITION NOW WITH DISCUSSION GUIDE FOR CHILDREN

A Story of a Promising Puppy
ISBN: 978-0-9826854-1-9
Copyright © 2010 by Leila Grandemange
Second Edition © 2011 by Leila Grandemange

First Printing December, 2010
Second Printing February, 2011

SunnyVille Publishing
P.O. Box 181, Goode, VA 24556
www.sunnyvillepublishing.com

Credits

All dogs photographed are Grandville Cavaliers, by Leila Grandemange • www.GrandvilleCavaliers.com

Assistance with photography:
Nichols Photography • pages 32, 33, 40, 41
Christy Johns • pages 24, 39

Cover design and interior layout by Christy Johns
CJ Designs, Virginia • www.CJDesigns.com
Revision layout by ED&M Design, Lynchburg, Virginia

IStockphoto image credits

©2010 iStockphoto Gary Godby
©2010 iStockphoto Gregor Buir
©2010 iStockphoto Megan Tamaccio
©2010 iStockphoto Roselyn Carr
©2010 iStockphoto Maljuk
©2010 iStockphoto Liudmila Chernova
©2010 iStockphoto dra_schwartz
©2010 iStockphoto Ekaterina Romanova
©2010 iStockphoto Denis Jr. Tangney
©2010 iStockphoto Eneri LLC
©2010 iStockphoto SilkenOne
©2010 iStockphoto Steven Foley
©2010 iStockphoto William Britten
©2010 iStockphoto Erik Enervold
©2010 iStockphoto Yauheni Attsetski

©2010 iStockphoto Alan Menzies
©2010 iStockphoto Ajay Shrivastava
©2010 iStockphoto Dzmitry Shpak
©2010 iStockphoto Anna Pakhomova
©2010 iStockphoto xyno
©2010 iStockphoto Darja Tokranova
©2010 iStockphoto Ela Kwasniewski
©2010 iStockphoto Dmitry Remesov
©2010 iStockphoto james steidl
©2010 iStockphoto ollo
©2010 iStockphoto JurgaR
©2010 iStockphoto Mark Richardson
©2010 iStockphoto Lisa Thornberg
©2010 iStockphoto Selahattin Bayram
©2010 iStockphoto gremlin

Sunny Ville
PUBLISHING
GOODE, VIRGINIA
Printed in the United States of America

This book is lovingly dedicated to

MY PRECIOUS DOGS

Thank you for sharing glimpses of God's unconditional
love—through joys, tears, laughter, and pain,
you have always been there for me!

Without a word, a dog taught me
the meaning of love . . .

Master Billy's House

Chapter One

A Promising Puppy

Once upon a time on a morning so chilly,

I was born a wee pup, to a Master named Billy.

I'm a Cavalier King Charles, "Star" is my name,

Short for "Starlight Reflections"—a show name with fame!

Told I was promising, a puppy with flair,

With love and attention, he raised me with care.

He had a large mirror, so fancy and old,

Before it I sat, my face to behold.

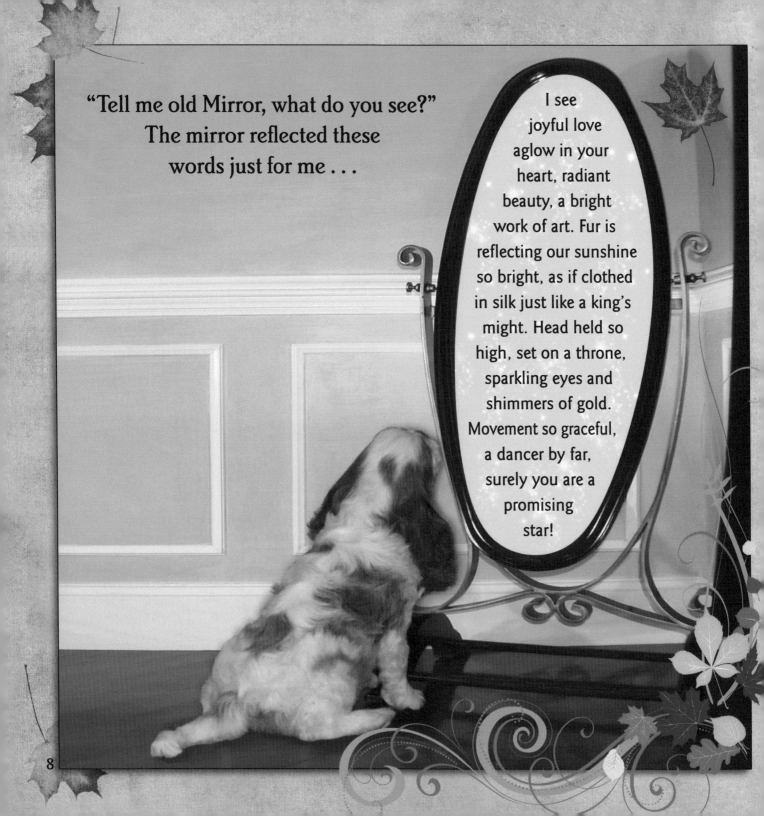

"Tell me old Mirror, what do you see?"
The mirror reflected these
words just for me . . .

I see joyful love aglow in your heart, radiant beauty, a bright work of art. Fur is reflecting our sunshine so bright, as if clothed in silk just like a king's might. Head held so high, set on a throne, sparkling eyes and shimmers of gold. Movement so graceful, a dancer by far, surely you are a promising star!

Beholding my beauty, this image so sweet,
Joy filled my being as I leaped to my feet.
Spinning in circles, I jumped to the sky,
I chased after balls, I felt I could fly!

With Billy I ran, I played all the days,
The things that he taught me were all filled with praise.
To obey was a game, I loved chasing sticks,
I learned very quickly, especially tricks!

Chapter Two

A Sad Day

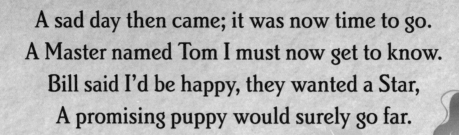

A sad day then came; it was now time to go.
A Master named Tom I must now get to know.
Bill said I'd be happy, they wanted a Star,
A promising puppy would surely go far.

So with hugs and a lick we each said goodbye,
Then one final word Master Bill spoke with pride:

"Some jewels of wisdom I really must share,
I've molded and taught him with the utmost care.
I was the potter, he was the clay—
Continue to mold him, I trust and I pray.

"Let love and patience guide you each hour,
Then watch as he blossoms, a beautiful flower.

"Heed my advice, he'll grow into a Star,

But don't leave out love, or he'll never go far."

Tom tried to listen but left in a hurry,

Dreaming of glory with his newfound puppy!

MASTER
TOM'S
HOUSE

CHAPTER THREE
Long Lonely Days

Tom seemed very nice, and he fed me well,
He brushed my coat, and loved my good smell.
But he wasn't too fond of playful hugs;
Perhaps he didn't like me, so I lay on my rug.

I tried to be chipper, as good as can be,
But each day Tom left to work around three.
Tom worked outside 'most all of the day,
So I sat alone with no one to play.

As puppies will do, I enjoyed a good chew,
I had my own fun tasting his shoe.
The day was too long, and though I tried to smile,
I couldn't hold my potty so I left a small pile.

Then off to my crate I drifted to sleep,
And waited for Tom, I couldn't wait to greet . . .

Joy filled my heart as I heard the door;
Running to greet Tom, I skidded on the floor.

Suddenly my heart sank, and fear gripped my spine,
As Tom's face changed, I hid just in time.

Tom began yelling something about shoes,
Then seeing my potty—that was bad news!

I got a spanking, and off to my crate.
Why did he yell? My heart seemed to ache!

CHAPTER FOUR
Changing Image

The days dragged on slowly as Tom tried to train me.

Frustration and anger came to him quickly.

I must be a failure, I must not be pretty,

I didn't hear kind words, as I did when with Billy.

But dog shows were different, and Tom seemed so proud,
Strutting and smiling, hoping to please the crowd!

We went 'round the ring, and trotted with the pros,
But if I didn't win, it seemed my heart froze.

A blue ribbon win brought cheers and favor,
Second ribbon or less, I was such a failure.

Peeking through my crate, seeing sadness in his eyes,
His hopes were all dashed, he wouldn't see the prize.

Master Tom grew so distant; I would never be his star.
Supposing he was right, I would never go far.

I no longer walked, I no longer played,
I just lay around, and I hoped for praise.

My tail stopped its wagging,
my fur grew so limp;
Curling my back,
now I even felt sick.
So I ran to a mirror, asking,
"What do you see?"
The mirror reflected,

Come sit
next to me . . .
An unhappy doggie,
no hope and no zeal,
Your eyes have no sparkle,
and life no appeal. Your fur
isn't shiny, you look a bit thin,
Your movement is slow, and
you don't want to spin. You
don't walk with pride,
no melody in your tail,
Your growth's almost
stunted, you seem
a bit frail.

My reflection brought tears,
a bad feeling inside,
I could no longer look,
and the sun seemed
to hide.

HOME
SWEET
HOME

CHAPTER FIVE
New Beginnings

The day came so soon, Tom found me a home,
Said I'd make a good pet and I'd not be alone.
Not even a tear was brought to his eye,
As I gave him a lick and said my goodbye.

Now worried thoughts danced in my mind—
Would they even love me; would they be kind?
Then I saw their faces with smiles big and wide,
And soon all my fears began to subside.

My new family held me,
we'd laugh and we'd play.
They taught me with patience
to learn and obey.

They lavished me with kisses,
spoiled me with toys;
As my toy basket grew,
each day brought new joys!

Walking with the Mistress
I held my head high,

My tail started wagging,
a sparkle in my eye!

People came to greet me,
I felt like a king,

They spoke to me sweetly,
I just wanted to sing!

Chapter Six

Reflections
of Glory

One day Tom returned; he stopped at the door,
Stunned to see such beauty greet him from the floor.
Tom then exclaimed, "Well, this dog is for show!"
And they all were amazed that he just didn't know.

"Why, this was your puppy," my family explained.
"You gave him away, and you're only to blame.
We've loved him and praised him, so now you can see,
He's grown up so pretty, I'm sure you'll agree."

Tom gave a big sigh, had an ache in his chest.
A champion is made when we give all our best.
What Tom seemed to forget was the best gift of all:
It's praise and it's love, no matter how small.

A puppy can't grow on good food alone,
Love makes him shine, until he's full grown.
Licking Tom's hand, I looked in his eyes.
I saw my reflection and beheld the prize.

A shiny blue ribbon, a trophy of gold,
I'm a winner each day, until I am old!

I ran to a mirror—could this be true?
The mirror reflected, "Believe it, it's you!"

Stunned by my beauty, I turned back to see,
But no one was there; yes, surely, it's me!

A bright shining Star, with love by my side,
My new family hugged me, saying, "He is our pride!"

That night in my bed, all warm and cuddly,
My heart full of love, I felt sort of bubbly.

Looking out my window,
the night seemed so bright,

A prayer came to mind as
I said my goodnight.

This Doggie's Prayer

Into your life I came one day, by chance or by will, I'm here to stay.

Little and furry, I brought you joy; young and untrained, trouble and spoil.

Don't get angry, don't dismay; I'll grow and change, don't give me away.

I don't speak your language, be patient I say;

I'll learn what you teach me; please train me, I pray.

I love to run, I love to play; please don't crate me all the day.

I need your love, I've grown so much; no longer a puppy, I still need your touch.

I love to eat, I'll munch what I may; but please remember I'll get fat one day.

Measure my food, and give water to drink,

I get awfully thirsty—my tongue will hang pink!

Check-ups and shots, I, too, need a doctor;

I might get sick; have you got a thermometer?

As time goes by I'll grow older and gray;

May all that I need come from you, I pray.

All that you give, I'll return even better;

This doggie's prayer is to love you forever!

And the day I must leave, hold me close, I pray;

I'll sleep in your arms and forever I'll stay.

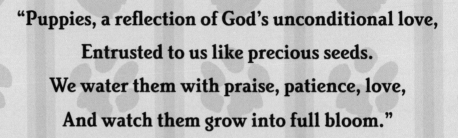

"Puppies, a reflection of God's unconditional love,
Entrusted to us like precious seeds.
We water them with praise, patience, love,
And watch them grow into full bloom."

— Leila Grandemange

To the Reader

A Story of a Promising Puppy is a delightful tale sharing the importance of responsible dog ownership; it also reveals the power of love to transform lives. Owning a dog is so much more than simply providing good food, water, and an occasional pat—it's a serious commitment involving preparation, time, training, nurture, and patience. These, like seeds, when planted and watered with love, have the ability to unlock the full potential in any living being!

I am constantly amazed at how my words, actions, and time invested into the lives of my children and dogs play a major role in how they develop. Star discovered his true worth when he finally received unconditional love! He was transformed and his beauty radiated for all to see.

It is my earnest prayer that each reader, young or old, will be inspired to extend this powerful gift of unconditional love to those around him. Like Star, I once felt unloved and lonely. Then one day, I discovered God's love and was transformed from the inside out! Dear Reader, God loves you unconditionally. Like Star, look into the mirror and see your beauty and worth.

"Believe it, it's YOU!"

Love is patient, love is kind. It does not envy, it does not boast, it is not proud. It does not dishonor others, it is not self-seeking, it is not easily angered, it keeps no record of wrongs. Love does not delight in evil but rejoices with the truth. It always protects, always trusts, always hopes, always perseveres. Love never fails.

—I Corinthians 13:4-8

About the Cavalier King Charles Spaniel

A Story of a Promising Puppy features a precious Cavalier King Charles Spaniel. For centuries, this breed was an inseparable companion to European nobility. Also referred to as "comforter spaniels," their gentle, affectionate nature and longing for a lap makes them ideal companions. Active, elegant, and friendly, this toy breed (13–18 pounds) with silky coat comes in four colors—Blenheim, Tricolor, Ruby, and Black and Tan. As part of the Toy group, they were recognized by the AKC in 1995.

PROMOTING RESPONSIBLE DOG OWNERSHIP

Please adopt, or choose your next puppy from a caring, responsible breeder.

For information about the Cavalier King Charles Spaniel
or to locate a breeder or rescue group, please contact:

Cavalier King Charles Spaniel Club USA, Inc. • www.ckcsc.org

American Cavalier King Charles Spaniel Club • www.ackcsc.org

For information about other breeds contact:

The American Kennel Club • www.akc.org

With Heartfelt Thanks . . .

To God, for creating such amazing love in a cuddly package of fur we call dog.

What a wildly wonderful world, God!
You made it all, with Wisdom at your side,
made earth overflow with your wonderful creations.

—Psalm 104:24 *The Message*

To my family, for your daily love, support, and input throughout this project.

To rescue organizations, you helped bring awareness into my world of the many sad situations some dogs endure—abuse, puppy mills, loneliness, neglect. Thank you for opening your hearts and homes and giving them a second chance.

ORDER INFORMATION

For additional copies, please contact
Sunny Ville Publishing
e-mail: info@sunnyvillepublishing.com
www.sunnyvillepublishing.com

He is your friend,
your partner, your defender, your dog.
You are his life, his love, his leader.
He will be yours, faithful and true,
to the last beat of his heart.
You owe it to him to be worthy of such devotion.

Author unknown

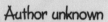

A Story of a Promising Puppy

DISCUSSION GUIDE

PURPOSE: *This guide was created to facilitate discussion with children in order to encourage responsible dog ownership. Our goal is to bring awareness of a dog's needs and find practical ways to meet those needs.*

Dear Parent or Educator,

The children of today are the dog owners of tomorrow. Owning a dog can be a fun and rewarding experience, yet children are often unaware of the responsibilities involved. By sharing the message of responsible dog ownership, we are investing in a bright future for our dogs. One child touched by Star's story might mean one more happy dog down the road. This is our motivation for discussing this story with any children who will lend us their eyes and ears!

After reading *A Story of a Promising Puppy* with your children, ask the following questions, taking time to listen and respond to their answers. The purpose is not to give the "correct" answers, but to guide them to think about the commitment involved in owning a dog. Ultimately, we would like the children to reflect on practical ways they can be sensitive to their dogs' needs in order to help their pets to grow into their full potential. You can adapt the questions to fit your target age group.

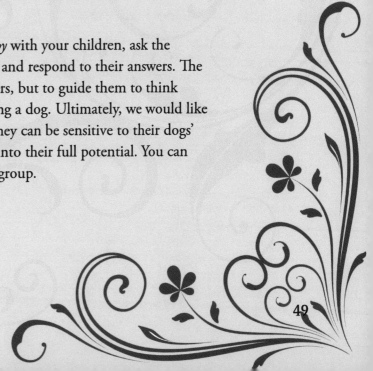

Here are some suggestions for questions which can be adapted for all ages:

1. Master Billy was a kind and responsible breeder. Describe how he cared for Star.

   Possible answers: he praised him and taught him many fun things; he was patient and kind...

2. How do you know Star was happy in Master Billy's home?

   Possible answers: wagging, jumping, leaping, chasing balls, the mirror said he was beautiful...

3. What wise advice did Master Billy give Tom regarding Star's future?

   Possible answers: be patient, don't leave out love...

4. Tom scolded Star for chewing his shoe and making potty in the house. How would you react if your dog did the same thing?

   Possible answers: I would not scold my dog. I would make sure he went out to potty more often. I would find him activities so he would not get bored.

5. At Tom's house, the mirror painted a sad picture of Star. How can you tell a dog is sad or bored?

   Possible answers: tail tucked between legs, head lowered, no desire to play, possible lack of appetite, whining, barking, anxious behavior, chewing furniture...

6. Tom could not give Star the time and attention he needed, and realized his home was not a "good fit." Before inviting a dog into your home, what can you do to make sure your home is a "good fit"?

   Possible answers: read a book about dogs and training, research the internet about different breeds, volunteer at the animal shelter, seek advice from other dog owners...

7. When Star finally finds his "forever" home, everything changes! Describe Star in his new home.

   Possible answers: we see him playing with toys, wagging and walking with his owner and greeting people. Star discovers he is a winner each day and is truly beautiful!

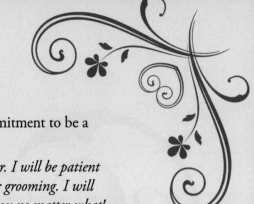

8. Write a letter to your dog, future dog, or to Star showing your commitment to be a responsible dog owner. Reread Star's prayer for ideas.

   Example: Dear _____ , I will do my best to be a responsible dog owner. I will be patient and kind. I will help train you, give you exercise, good food, and regular grooming. I will play with you and not leave you alone too long. Most of all, I will love you no matter what! (Encourage children to share this with their parents.)

Follow-up activities:

1. Have children make a list of items they may need in order to prepare their home for a dog. Have them cut out images from magazines of those items (beds, bowls, brushes, collar, name tag…) and make a collage.
2. Ask children to bring a photo of their pet (dog, cat, bird, hamster…) and "show and tell" how they specifically care for their pets' needs.

Option for digging deeper:

Ask children to share or write about what it means to love "unconditionally."

Ideas for prompts:

   Conditional love says, "I will love you IF…(you are good, pretty, successful…)"

   Unconditional love says, "I will love you no matter what…"

Ask children to find expressions of conditional and unconditional love in the story.

Ask, "Which type of love would you like to show your dog and others in your life?"

If you are a parent reading to your children, you might like to share how your love for them is unconditional. Give examples and end by reinforcing that you love them because they are special and beautiful in your eyes!

CPSIA information can be obtained
at www.ICGtesting.com
225724LV00001B